We Like Colors!

Disney PRESS

New York • Los Angeles

D1455314

Lightning likes red.
He is as red as a rose.

Sally likes blue.
She is as blue as the sky.

Mater likes brown.
He is as brown as the soil.

Fillmore likes green.
He is as green as the cactus

Luigi likes yellow.
He is as yellow as the sun.

Ramone likes purple.
He is as purple as the night.

We like colors!